Paul's Cat

Jameson Currier

Chelsea Station Editions

New York

Paul's Cat
Story and Illustrations by Jameson Currier
Copyright © 2022 and 2026 by Jameson Currier

Book design by Peachboy Distillery & Designs
Published by Chelsea Station Editions
www.chelseastationeditions.com
info@chelseastationeditions.com

Print ISBN: 978-1-937627-81-2
Library of Congress Control Number: 2022938195
First published: 2022
Second Edition: 2026

Paul's Cat

Down the Stairwell

Jay had promised Paul that he would look after his cat. He'd walked several blocks from the subway stop to reach Paul's apartment atop a five-floor building in a risky part of town. He used the keys Paul had given him, unlocked the street door, checked the mail at the boxes in the lobby, and walked up the stairs to Paul's top-floor apartment.

As he fumbled with the keys on the keyring to find the right one for the door lock, Jay heard the meowing of the cat behind the door. He found the key and unlocked the bolt lock with a snap and the door cracked open. Paul's cat pushed its way through the door and darted into the hallway before Paul had removed the key from the lock. The cat looked back at Jay, swished its tail, and ran down the stairs.

"Kitty," Jay called out. "Come back! Kitty!"

Jay looked down the stairwell to the mid-floor landing. The cat stopped, looked up at Jay, swished its tail, and continued downward.

"No, no, no," Jay said, going down the stairs, following the cat, hoping to get close enough so that he could scoop it up and take it back upstairs to the apartment.

The cat repeated the scenario. Down the steps, stop, look back up, swish the tail, scamper down the steps. Again and again. Jay had to stop and catch his breath. There was no air circulating in the building stairwell. And there came a point where he was certain he had descended more than five flights. His mind flashed through worst case scenarios. The cat might escape into the street and be hit by a taxi or a bus. The cat might never be found and become homeless and a stray, if it could survive on the streets. Or starve and perish. More than once, Jay wondered how he would explain it if the cat escaped and never returned.

Down a floor, then another, with no end in sight. There were signs on the apartment doors Jay had never noticed before: No Muff Diving. Pants Optional. Pizza Deliveries Only. Dogs Must Be

6

Carried. Too Late to Turn Back Now. At times he felt like he was losing his balance. Other times he had to grasp the handrail to make sure he was not in a dream.

Finally, the stairs stopped. The cat was twitching its tail in front of a partially cracked door and then, deliberately, slipped through it.

Jay looked through the crack into the bright room. It appeared to be a basement laundry room. He opened the door wider and saw the cat on the other side of the room, slipping through another partially cracked door and disappearing out of sight.

Inner Beauty

As Jay began to cross the room, he realized it was not a laundry room. The washers were not washers but white vanities, ringed by mirrors and bright, exposed light bulbs. Costumes hung from rolling racks. There were trays and jars and tubes of make-up and cremes atop every flat surface. He seemed to have walked into a backstage dressing room.

Something yapped viciously near his ankle. Jay jumped. A tiny chihuahua wearing a rhinestone collar barked at him from beneath a chair. One cloudy eye stared accusingly upward beneath a white wave of hair. A large person stepped in front of Jay and said in a deep, angry voice, "Who you?"

"Nobody. Don't mind me."

The large person stepped closer to Jay. The person was much taller and wider than Jay and wearing so much black that Jay thought the lights had gone out.

"You ain't nobody. Ain't you learnt that?"

Jay stepped back so that he could see a chest, a neck, and a face. Or at least portions of them.

"You lost, pretty boy?"

The chihuahua barked again. A high-pitched snappy yap. The large person bent down and coaxed the dog from beneath the chair and lifted it up, pressing it to its chest. Or bosom.

"Cha Cha don't trust nervous men," the large person said. Then, without a beat, added, "I bet you were bullied for those ears."

"My ears?"

"And that nose."

"My nose?"

Each time the large person said these statements to Jay, the large person's ears grew larger and the person's nose grew bigger and wider.

Jay touched his ears and nose to make sure nothing had changed for him. It hadn't.

But there was an ambiguity to the constant morphing of the large person from pretty and feminine to muscular and masculine. The eyes were large and dark and ringed with lashes that looked like claws. Black hair was pulled back from

10

the round face and a tall conical hat made the large person look comically taller. Jay didn't know whether to be confused or worried. And it was not the right time to offer criticism on the outfit the large person was wearing. Pink satin with black leather and studs were a bit cliché in any season.

"I bet you were bullied for being too pretty," the person said with a harsh, raspy mannish voice.

The comment hit a memory for Jay: two boys taunting him in his high school hallway.

The large person seized on the flicker of recognition, becoming bigger and prettier and stepping closer to Jay. Jay was now aware there were other persons in the room, each rising from their chairs at their dressing room tables and inching suspiciously toward him. They were also dressed in pink satin and black leather outfits. They seemed to be one moment a gang of chorus girls at an underground nightclub, then a street gang of tough boys, then, as they surrounded the leader, a group of unfinished drag queens in black net stockings and leotards embellished with sequins—all of them part men, part women—morphing and shifting just as the largest one did.

"I'm just getting the cat," Jay said and pointed to the door at the opposite wall, even though he knew it was bad manners to point. "It ran through the room. I just need to catch the cat."

"Cat?" the large one bellowed. "You chasin' pussy? Girls, he chasin' pussy!"

"He chasin' pussy!" the others echoed. It inspired them to chant the phrase and strike poses, as if they were posing for fashion photographs.

"There's a lot of pussy in here. Why does a pretty boy like you want to find something better?"

Jay realized the conical hat was not a hat at all but a wig in the shape of an upturned funnel with a tiny tiara in the middle. Everyone was wearing wigs and tiaras. They were all drag queens, he decided. He relaxed a bit, thinking crazy queens in pointy wigs and little crowns were less worrisome than an army of angry giants wearing funnel hats.

"I don't mean to be rude. The cat. He just ran into the room and out through that door. I just need to get him."

The dog growled. Jay imagined the cloudy eye blinking.

"What's the cat mean to you?"

"It belongs to a friend. Upstairs."

"Cats don't belong to nobody."

Paul's cat appeared briefly at the far side of the room and slipped through another door. "There," Jay pointed. The dog responded with a double bark.

"You can't just walk through this room and out that door. Especially that door. Not like that."

"Like what?" Jay asked.

"Like that. Pretty boy with no armor. You got a name?"

"Jay."

The large drag queen bounced the tiny dog in her arms. "This here Cha Cha. And I ain't Miss Thing for nuthin'. It takes years and years of experience and hard knocks and hiding the candy to walk through that door. We don't just wake up beautiful and talented and ultra-special."

"I don't have that kind of time."

"You're not even dressed right. What kind of style is this?"

Jay had neither money or need for nice clothes. He was dressed in jeans and a plain T-shirt. "Style?"

"I spent hours making my outfit. Sister, here, spent thousands of dollars on hers. Of course, she don't look as beautiful as I do, but then you have to spend money where you have to spend it best."

"You don't understand. I just need the cat. I promised..."

"You promised? Well, why didn't you say so in the first place. If this was a promise!"

Miss Thing turned and clapped to the chorus group. "Girls, we gottta give this pretty boy some sparkle so he can catch his pussy!"

The group surrounded Jay. The attention and tickles felt silly. At one moment Jay thought his leg had been bent behind his neck.

"Voilà," the large person said and held a mirror in front of Jay. Two smaller drag queens were clipping a tiara to Jay's hair. The large queen had draped a satin sash across his chest that read "WINNER!"

"I don't know who I am," Jay said. He realized he was holding a scepter encrusted with sequins.

"Of course you do," the large one said. "You are your inner self."

Jay felt his inner—and outer—self frowning. This wasn't who he was at all. But he had to get through the door so he knew he had to humor the giant drag queen.

"Now show me your walk," Miss Thing demanded.

"My walk?"

"Your walk. Convince me that you deserved that sash and scepter."

Jay took a step and felt his shoe scuff the floor. He lifted his ankle and tried again.

"You gotta use your hips and knees," the large person said. "Extend your spine. Be proud!"

Jay tried again and realized his feet were stuck to the floor. "You want me to do this in sneakers?"

Miss Thing was not happy. "Girl, you got some natural beauty, but that ain't enough. You gotta practice!"

Jay looked down at his feet. "Is this necessary?" he asked. His eyes welled up with tears. No, this wasn't him at all. He had no sense of adventure. No sense of risk or pursuit of happiness. He wished Paul was here. Paul would have thrown his head back and laughed and learned how to dance in heels. He would have instantly become best friends with everyone in the room.

"Some people say that you become a stronger person in drag," Miss Thing said. "A different person. A mightier soul. That ain't so, sweetheart. You gotta be tough no matter who you are or what you're wearing."

"It might help if he had a name," one of the chorus queens said.

"A name?"

"Kitty Litter," a queen suggested.

"Cat de Blow."

"Not at all," the large one said. "Girls, meet Missin' Pussy."

The group laughed and the laughter was oddly infectious, even if Jay was the butt of a joke. Miss Thing reached out and adjusted the crooked tiara on Jay's head. Up close, Jay noticed exhaustion beneath the makeup. Fine lines beneath the powder. A slight tremor in the fingers holding the growling dog. Just as he was wondering about the mental health of an overly large drag queen, she leaned into him and whispered, "You okay?"

The question startled Jay. Nobody had asked him that in a long time. "I'm fine."

"No," she answered. "You ain't." She clapped her hands, as if making a command. "You don't walk through certain doors unless you got the confidence to become somebody first. Now, you one of us. Go on out there and wow 'em."

As Jay walked across the room and through the doorway, he felt his confidence fading. He entered a long, dark hallway, and walked toward a light that bent around the corner. Suddenly, he realized that he was walking across an empty stage wearing a tiara and a sash and carrying a scepter. There was a microphone center stage and which was where Jay stopped. He looked out at the rows of theater seats. They were empty with the exception of one. A man was seated fourth row center, his arms folded across his chest. He was bald and had a black and gray stubble that circled his jaw and resembled a goatee-in-progress. His black frame eyeglasses were balanced atop his bald skull. Jay wondered how many years it had taken him to perfect that talent.

"It helps to be on time," the man said. "If you want to be taken seriously."

Outer Skills

"Your resume says your favorite class was band," the seated man said to Jay. "What instrument did you play?"

"I don't have a resume," Jay answered. "I haven't had a resume in years."

"But I have it right here. It says your favorite class in high school was band, but it doesn't say what instrument you played. What instrument?"

"Clarinet."

"Well, that makes sense."

"Why does that make sense?"

"Because I said it does. I see you were an English major and the editor of the annual. And you're familiar with story structure and stereotypes. But can you explain the Great Vowel Shift?"

"I'm not familiar with that."

"Of course not, and that explains everything. Your skills are lacking."

Jay felt uneasy with the pageant trappings that he was wearing. He thought about removing them, but his annoyance persisted. "I'm not looking for a job. I'm just trying to find a cat."

"I see. That must be why it says you are perfect boyfriend material."

"It doesn't say that. Now I know you don't have my resume."

"I don't understand why these resumes never detail your lack of skills. Have you ever used a table saw?"

"A table saw? No. I can't say that I have ever had a reason to."

"Can you change a flat tire or jump a battery?"

"I don't have a car. I live in the city. I don't have a reason for a car. And I don't see how any of this is relevant."

"Relevant? And you think you're husband material?"

The question opened a wound. A history of Jay's failed relationships.

"First date. First date. First date. Sex. Sex. Sex. But never a second date. What makes you think you are worthy of a husband? Or to be a husband."

Jay did not answer.

"That's another matter that's not addressed on this piece of paper. Top or bottom?"

"I'm not here for you to make me feel miserable," Jay said. "I'm not looking for a husband. Or a boyfriend or a date or a trick. I am trying to find Paul's cat."

"And who is this Paul and what does he mean to you?"

Another wound opened. Jay kept silent. Out of the corner of his eye, he saw a movement at the back of the theater. It was Paul's cat. The cat was stalking something.

"Cat got your tongue?"

"Yes, I'm afraid it does."

Jay exited the stage and found the stairs that lead into the theater auditorium. "Kitty," he whispered, running toward the place where he had seen the cat.

The cat looked at Jay, swished its tail, and disappeared behind a curtain.

Fortune or Future?

Behind the curtain was a set of stairs that led to another door. Jay ripped off the sash and tossed it with the scepter into a dark corner. He followed the cat down the steps and watched it slip through the crack of another partially opened door. The door led to a dark alley. The cat leapt to a windowsill and treaded its way around a row of garbage cans to a set of black iron stairs that led to the door of a building at the end of the alley. A man was walking up the stairs and opened the door. Jay called out, "Kitty! Wait!" but the cat followed the man inside the building.

Jay felt defeated, certain he'd never be able to find the cat. He walked down the dark alley and up the black iron steps. There was no buzzer for the door but it opened when Jay grasped the handle. Inside was a small lobby where a person with a long face and wearing a dark turban was seated behind a counter that was encased by clear plastic panels.

Beside the counter was a list of rules and a sign that read MEMBERS ONLY.

Jay leaned down toward the small window opening of the plastic panel and asked the long-faced person, "Did you see a cat come through here?"

"I see cats and dogs and frogs and princes. I don't cast judgement."

"But did you see a cat?" Jay asked. He scrutinized the person trying to determine a gender. There was eye shadow and fake eyelashes and ringlets of dark hair peeking from beneath the turban. But there was also a wispy moustache and chin hairs. "Do you mind if I take a look inside?"

"Members only," the person said in a high-pitched voice and pointed to the sign.

Jay could still not make a conclusion about the person. "How do I become a member?" he asked.

"We don't discriminate. All are welcome."

"So, it's okay to go inside and look around?"

"Sorry, members only."

"How do I become a member?"

"You have to know the answers."

"Okay," Jay said. "What are the questions?"

"The questions are always changing."

"So how can I know the answers?"

"That is the answer."

"Then I can go inside?"

"Not like that."

"What's wrong with this?"

"It's not the future."

"The future?"

"Fashion forward."

"Do I need to wear what you're wearing?

"I'm already out of date. That's why I'm out here telling fortunes and not inside experiencing the future."

"But the future is never about fortunes. No one can predict the future."

"That's prejudicial. Some fortunes are good. Others are not. The future is the next thing."

"You make the future sound depressing."

"It's as depressing as the past."

"I need to go through that door," Jay said. "I need to find the cat. That's my future."

"No," the person said. "I've seen your future."

"Oh... And?"

"You will be cut open and put back together again."

The weight of the person's prophecy landed against Jay's chest and forehead. "It's already happened," he said. "That's the past."

"No. Not heartbreak. This time it will be physical. You'll be unprepared."

Jay watched the person's eyes flicker with hurt. He stepped back from the counter, trying not to display his frustration and concern. His scalp itched and when he touched his hair he realized he still wore the tiara the drag queens had pinned there. Jay twisted it off his head.

"You want it?" he asked the person and slipped the tiara beneath the plastic window opening.

The person was surprised by the gift. "It's beautiful."

"With beauty comes pain," Jay said. "I can see the future too."

The person twirled the tiara on the counter and said, "There's another way inside."

"Another way?"

"It's a little more work."

"Than... this?" Jay asked.

"This door," the person said and pointed to a door beside Jay he had not noticed before. "Employees only. There are showers. Lockers. Uniforms on the shelves. You will need to work while you look for your cat. Work your way to the top."

"Deal," Jay said.

"It will not be an easy path."

"The future never is."

Perfect Potential

A buzzer sounded and Jay walked through the opened door and into a room with rows of lockers. Small lockers on top of other small lockers. Long lockers next to other long lockers. Standing in front of a mirror he saw the tiara had unsettled his hair. Jay was close to giving up on finding Paul's cat.

Jay had never felt at ease in a locker room. He was the last person in junior high to hit puberty but the first one to get an erection in the showers. It was the reason why he had joined the band. If you played in the band you didn't have to take gym class. You didn't have to be hit by a dodge ball. You didn't have to be standing in the outfield wondering if you would catch a tiny ball flying through the air. Paul loved the locker rooms. He loved the showers and saunas and the dangling and the ogling.

Jay slipped into a shower stall and began to hurriedly undress and wash. He dried off without looking at himself in the mirror and left the wet towel on the bench. He felt the vibrations of dance music before he heard the deep beating of music playing far away. And he was aware that he was being watched. A short man with giant eyes and oversized muscles was scrutinizing Jay.

"You have great potential," the man said.

"Perfect proportions," the man added.

Jay tried to ignore the man. He found the shelf of uniforms. They were T-shirts and shorts. He found his sizes and slipped them on. The music seemed to get louder and softer, louder and softer.

"You just need work," the man said. He had followed Jay to the shelves and then back to the bench. "Then you wouldn't have to hide your body all the time."

"You'd be a god," he added.

"A god amongst gods."

"Thanks, but I'm kind of in a hurry," Jay said.

"I can put you on the expedited track," the man answered. He opened the door of a nearby long locker. Inside was an assortment of bottles and jars on a variety of shelves. He pointed to a blue bottle. "This blue one will do biceps nicely. Make them peak." He pointed to another bottle. "The pink creme. Triceps. Green pills, tree trunk thighs. The speckled brown pills will widen your shoulders."

One bottle caught Jay's attention. Its label read "DE GAY" Jay pointed to the bottle. "What does this one do?" he asked.

"That's the pill that will make you straight."

The man reached for the bottle and shook it. There was no sound. He twisted off the lid and showed the empty bottle to Jay. "Obviously, one of our most popular. I could get a special delivery for you."

"I'm happy with the way I am," Jay said.

"Oh, surely not!" the man answered. "You'll never catch someone with..."

"What? With what? What's wrong with me?"

The man was distracted by something on the other side of the room. "It says on the rules, 'No Pets Allowed'. Is that your cat?"

Jay looked and saw Paul's cat. "Kitty!"

The cat looked at Jay, swished its tail, and darted into the hallway.

Members Only

The hall opened to a staircase that rose up to an enormous room the size of an airplane hangar, dark except for spotlights spinning across an empty floor. The Members Only club was a dance club. Music thumped and beat and kept time with the changing, swirling light show. Jay saw the cat skitter across the floor. As he crossed the room to chase the cat the music changed to a new song, a mirror ball descended from the ceiling, and the spotlights rotated their lights, sending reflections around the room. The area was suddenly filled with dancers. Men in jeans and T-shirts, some revolving so seriously they had shed their shirts. White smoke moved up from vents in the floor and down from the ceiling. Jay paused, lost in a nostalgic moment of when he had once been enchanted by the experience of visiting this kind of paradise.

When Jay reached the other side of the dance floor, he noticed the cat climbing a set of stairs.

A young man with dark skin and floppy hair stopped Jay from stepping onto the stairs. He was dressed as Jay was, in employee shorts and T-shirt.

"You can't go up there like that," the young man said to Jay.

"Like what?"

"Like that. This is the VIP room. You know what that means?"

"No, what?"

"You can't go up there like that."

Jay looked at the young man, tried to catch his eyes, but the young man's gaze was too wide and skittish to remain connected. "But I'm dressed exactly like you are," Jay said.

"Not exactly," the young man replied. He took a sleeve of Jay's T-shirt and began to rip it off. He ripped the other sleeve. From somewhere a set of scissors materialized and he cut off the bottom of the shirt so that Jay's navel showed.

"There," he said. Jay noticed that the young man's shirt was also ripped and shredded. The young man was at least a decade younger than Jay, or so Jay thought.

"I'm not sure I can pull this off," Jay said.

"You've got nice legs. Very retro."

Jay wasn't sure how to respond to the compliment.

"It's different," Jay said. "It was a different time. I feel different."

"Just listen to the music," the young man said. "Let the music lead you. Doesn't it make you want to be here, part of it, never anywhere else?"

Jay remained silent, searching for more reminders of himself in the disco. The young man unhooked the velvet rope that blocked the upstairs passage to the VIP room. "You didn't do the drugs, did you?" he asked Jay.

Jay remained quiet, trying to process if the young man meant drugs then or drugs now.

"Didn't you get training?"

"Training?"

"VIP training."

"I'm just..."

"You take the drink order. Never look anyone in the eyes. Give the order to the bartender. And stay sober as long as you can."

Upstairs there were clusters of men and women seated in banquettes and couches positioned around low tables. The music was underwhelming, but the conversations were rattling and punctuated with outbursts of laughter. Jay scanned the room for Paul's cat but it was nowhere to be seen. He had no intention of doing any work, avoiding the tables and groups. He had one purpose: find the cat and take him back to the apartment.

Jay looked beneath the tables, but the cat was nowhere. He walked to a railing and saw that the VIP room was a balcony that overlooked the large dance floor. Below, in the dancing crowd, a shirtless man danced with fans, twirling, swirling, flapping, and fanning. The sight kept Jay mesmerized and trapped in the past. He remembered how effortless it used to be. How happy it was to be liberated from a life he had been trying to escape and how fortunate he felt to be discovering himself and a new city at the same time.

It was fun until it wasn't fun anymore—when the rent came due and he was alone and worried, or moving from one guy to the next, looking for stability. A future. Or anything to keep him afloat.

He turned and looked back into the VIP area— to break the hold the past still held on him—and saw the young man who had helped him downstairs cleaning glasses from a table area that was suddenly empty but filling up with new customers. Without emotion, the young man emptied the ash trays and stacked the glasses on the small tray, balancing the trash and carrying it across the room. It reminded Jay of how hard it had been to accept the fact that he was probably not going to be an actor or dancer or singer or someone who belonged in a VIP room, but someone who had to take whatever job came along to make ends meet. That was when Jay saw the young man put the tray down and approach a large person sitting at a small table.

"Who you calling a dog?" a voice boomed through the private area.

Jay approached the table and saw it was Miss Thing holding a trembling Cha Cha.

"Tell him," Miss Thing waved to Jay. "Tell him I am an international beauty."

"There are no pets allowed here," the young man said.

"Who's got a pet? I don't got no pet. This here is my life. My soul." Miss Thing looked at Jay. "Tell him. Tell him Cha Cha is pure love."

The dog sneered at Jay. Before Jay could respond Paul's cat jumped up onto to the table and quickly skittered away. Cha Cha wriggled his way out of Miss Thing's embrace and was off chasing the cat.

"Kitty!" Jay said and set out after the cat and the dog.

Subconscious Conscience

Miss Thing was a loud chaser. She waved her arms and stomped her feet, yelling "Cha Cha! Cha Cha come here!" Under other circumstances, it might have made Jay laugh, but now he worried the dog would terrorize the cat and Miss Thing might create a panic.

When Jay reached the hallway where he had last seen the cat, it was empty. It was dark and carpeted, dim pin lights near the seams of the floor and the walls kept the perspective of a narrow way until Jay was surrounded by darkness and each step was deeper into blackness. The music had faded away. Jay thought he heard Miss Thing behind him, but he stopped and listened. There were groans and whispers and sighs and heavy breathing. Had he reached a backroom? he thought next, but then wondered if he was only hearing his own breathing and his sneakers moving across the carpet. A few steps later, the pin lights at the floor reappeared.

At the end of the hallway Jay could see someone seated in a chair. Closer, he saw it was a man. He was much older than the young men working and dancing in the club. As Jay approached, he could make out the old man's gray hair, a balding scalp, and the deep, fleshy rings beneath the man's tiny eyes.

"Can I get you a drink, sir?" Jay asked the man to break the tension.

"A drink?" the man echoed. "What is a drink when it is the soul that is malnourished?"

Jay stood still and quiet, not wanting to be disrespectful. "Do you need help?" he asked the man.

"Help?" the man echoed.

Jay thought the man might be drunk. Or high. Or sick. "I can help you downstairs. Help you get a taxi."

"I'm supposed to be the one helping," the old man said.

"I don't mind," Jay said.

"Mind? Of course you mind."

"No, really. I can help you if you need help."

"I'm the helper," the old man said. "My work is here."

"Here?" Jay echoed. All he saw was the man, the chair, and the darkness.

"I'm the conscience relegated to the subconscious."

The man was still and quiet, then suddenly broke into a fit of high-pitched laughter. "Look closely," the man said, when his laughter had subsided. "Two doors." He waved his arms at his side. Jay saw that the old man was seated in a chair between two doors. "One door leads to pleasure. All the pleasure you can want and have right now. Physical pleasure—sex, drugs—or emotional pleasures—love, desire, companions. The other door leads to knowledge. A long, hard, painful path to knowledge. And we all know that knowledge doesn't always lead to success. With knowledge comes the acceptance of responsibility, suffering, depression. And with pleasure comes pain, regret, depression, and illness. So, which one would you choose?"

"I'm not here to make a choice, sir," Jay said. "I'm here to help."

"As am I."

"I'm trying to find a cat. I saw a cat run down this hallway, so I am here for the cat."

"A cat?"

"A cat."

"I did see a cat," the old man said. "Just a few moments ago. It went through a door."

"Which door?" Jay asked.

"Which door?" the man echoed.

"Which door?"

"The cat has already made its decision."

"Which door?" Jay asked. "Which door did the cat take?"

"That would mean betraying a decision. A breach of confidentiality."

"No, it would be helping me find the cat."

"Helping?"

"Helping. Doing your job. I promised to help the cat."

"A cat?"

"A cat."

"Even if I were to tell you what door the cat took, it would not reveal the cat's fate. For every action there is a reaction no matter what door is chosen. Each door has its consequences."

"I understand the consequences," Jay said. "I'm here to get the cat."

"The cat is your future, then," the old man said. "Wouldn't it be great if we could reduce all of life to chasing a cat."

"You're being insulting now."

"Me? I'm here to help."

"I am trying to help a cat. You could help me find the cat."

"My rates are high," the old man said. "Hourly. No pro bono."

Jay refused to give up. And he had no money to pay an old man who might or might not be able to help him find Paul's cat. He quickly decided to change the conversation. "What if I told you I had already been through those doors?" he said to the old man. "Both of them."

"I'd ask you to tell me the stories."

"Then you would need to pay me," Jay said. "My stories are not free."

The old man did not flinch. "But I would help you understand your stories. And for that I would need to be compensated."

Now Jay laughed. "What makes you think I don't understand my own life? You're being presumptuous."

"And you're being insulting. Where are your manners? You're supposed to treat your elders with respect."

Jay stood quiet and still, then said, "Can I get you something to drink, sir?"

The man widened his eyes. "It would be a pleasure," the old man said, waving his hand toward that door.

The Pool of Memory

Jay opened the door to pleasure. Light filtered into the hallway and he saw that the old man had disappeared. He stepped through the door of pleasure and into a room, slipping off a shoe to keep the door from locking shut behind him. He saw that the door of knowledge led to the same room as the door of pleasure and he laughed at the joke.

Before him was a pool. Stadium size, with lanes marked off for swimming laps. Around the pool was a path of tiles. At the other end of the pool there was a stone bench. Paul's cat sat on the bench, looking across the water at Jay.

Before Jay had a chance to walk around the path of the pool to the bench and the cat, the door clicked shut. Someone had dislodged the shoe. And at the same time the door locked, the path around the pool disappeared. The only way to the bench and the cat was to swim across the pool.

Fate or consequences? Jay wondered, as he took off the other shoe and his socks. He had made a promise. He had come this far. He took off the ripped T-shirt and waded down the steps that led into the water, the smell of chlorine drifting up to his nose. The water was cold, then warmed. He walked toward the cat until his feet no longer touched the bottom of the pool. He had never been a confident swimmer, abandoning lifeguard training as a teenager when he refused to dive to retrieve a brick from the bottom of a pool.

Jay felt a current moving through the water, a wave followed by another wave. He remembered a time when he and Paul were at a beach; they had been floating and bobbing and chatting and laughing and realized that they had drifted too far from shore. Paul panicked and they began to swim toward shore. The waves breached around them, pulling them under. Jay remembered being pulled underwater, unable to surface because of the force of the current. He remembered thinking, "Not now, not now, not here, no, no, no," until he finally surfaced and gasped for air.

Jay followed the waves to the side of the pool, pushing back his growing fear, and used the cement lip to make his way down to the other end, hand by hand by hand, until he reached the bench and the cat.

He pulled himself out of the pool. Relieved, he stood and took a towel that was beside the cat and dried himself off. The cat looked up at Jay and then away. Beside the towel was a set of clothes: jeans, T-shirt, socks, and a pair of sneakers. Jay shook the water out of his hair and ears and slipped out of the wet employee shorts. He dressed into the clothes, understanding that they had always been his to find.

Jay sat beside the cat and reached over and petted it between the ears. The cat squinted its eyes. Jay leaned down and began to lace up the sneakers when the cat jumped off the bench. To the sides of the bench were hallways. Jay watched the cat prance down the hallway, swish its tail, and look back at him, as if commanding Jay to follow.

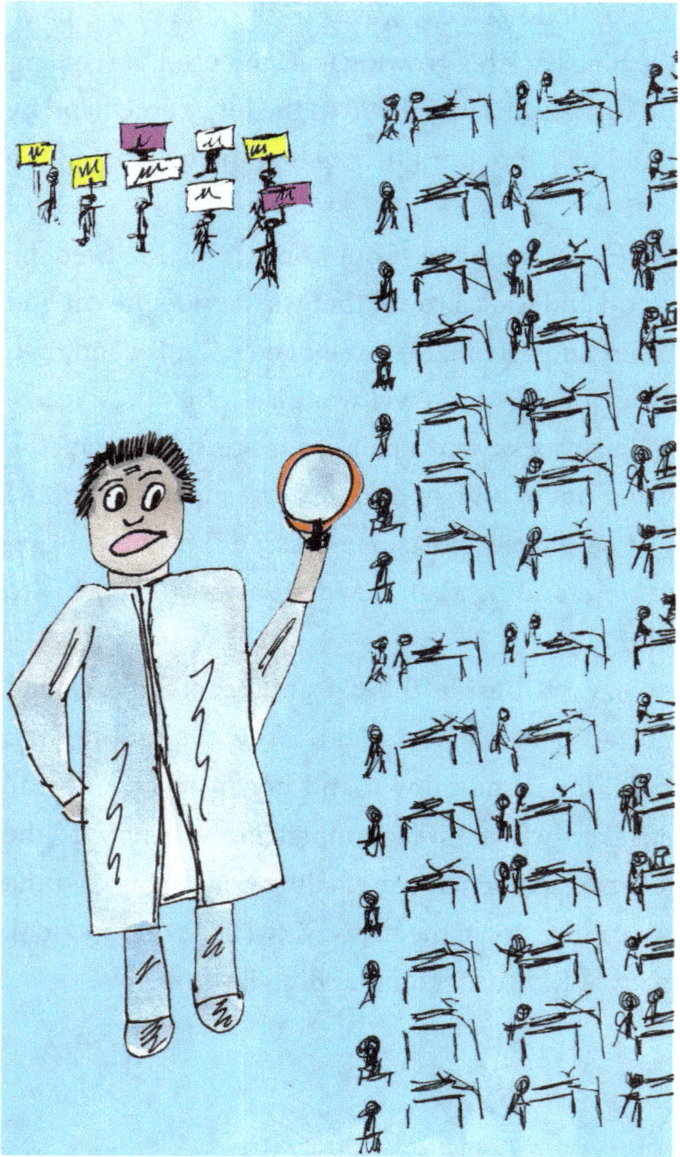

Sobbing or Screaming?

Jay followed the cat down the long corridor. The hallway opened to a longer room. A large woman wearing a white coat was in front of Jay, with mannish features and short brown hair, watching him approach. "Sobbing or screaming?" she asked Jay tersely.

"What?"

"What are you here for?" she asked Jay tersely. "Sobbing or screaming?"

Jay looked away from her to the room. It was a long, large room, full of rows of hospital beds. "What are you here for?" she asked him again. "Sobbing or screaming?"

"I'm just..."

Each hospital bed was occupied by a young man. The patients were attached to IV lines and catheters. Nurses padded up and down each of the aisles in white shoes and white coats.

"No one is just just. You either end up sobbing or screaming. If you're gonna be a noisy sobber you have to go to the Wailing Room. If you're gonna scream you need to go to Screamers Hall. It's too disruptive if you are noisy in here."

In the distance, at the end of the long room, Jay saw Paul's cat had reached a bed and leapt up on it and was sitting at the feet of a patient.

"This is the right place," he said to the large woman. Jay began walking through the room, toward the cat and the bed at the back of the room. The room grew longer as he proceeded toward the cat and the bed. He glanced down the rows of hospital beds. The patients were not the young men he thought he had seen from the front of the room. They were logs, with broken limbs and charred bark, twisting their twigs into the air, fluids seeping from their torsos. On closer look he could see the logs were thin and covered in reddish-blue lesions and bruises.

Jay lost his nerve and then got it back with a deep breath of air. The large woman followed him. "You want a mirror?" she asked Jay. "I gotta mirror that you can use that lets you see them without their sores. Peak of youth and tip-top health."

Jay stopped by a bed. He thought he recognized something about one of the logs. Something of someone he knew long ago. The nurse stopped beside him and held up a mirror that reflected the log. Jay looked into the mirror. It was Mark. Funny, goofy, talented Mark. Jay turned away from the mirror and walked to the bed, placing his hand on the rough scaly bark of the log.

"Is there anything you need?" Jay asked the log. Of course there was no response. Jay went to a night stand beside the bed, dampened a wash rag in a basin of warm water, and returned to the log. He placed the damp rag against the log. "Better?"

The damp rag was like a conductor of memories. Jay stood there for a few minutes, remembering conversations he had with Mark. He heard a cough and noticed something familiar about another log. He walked to the bed, dampened a wash rag, and placed it against the log. It was Dave. Neurotic, brilliant Dave.

Jay moved from bed to bed, astonished by the number of young men and his memories of them.

All the time, he kept his view of the cat in the distance, sitting on a bed at the end of the room.

"I've got rose-tinted glasses," the nurse said, still patiently following Jay. "The families use them a lot."

"This is good," Jay said, then turned back to the nurse. "No, of course, it's not *good*, but it reminds me that this is a part of who I was... Who I am."

When he reached the bed where the cat was sitting, he thought, "Why? Why do I have to go through this again?" The pain was still fresh.

He dampened a washrag and placed it against the log in the last bed. "Jay will know what to do," he heard Paul say.

"But I don't know what to do," Jay said.

"Of course, you do," Paul answered. "You're here."

A noisy sound began to fill the room—a light tapping that became a click-click-stomp-stomp of footfalls on the linoleum floor. The nurse left Jay's side and marched toward the front of the room, yelling at the assembling crowd—"You can't just barge into here! Where are your manners? Screamers to the Screamers Hall. Sobbers to the Wailing Room."

The nurse was not successful at holding back the crowd. They swarmed around her, chanting "Fight Back, Fight Now," and carrying signs that read "Where is Your RAGE?" and "United in ANGER!" The nurse was lost and the crowd pressed deeper into the ward. At the front of the activists was Miss Thing and her chorus of drag queens. Cha Cha was peeking out of a shoulder bag painted with the words, "FIGHT FOR LIFE!" The queens marched and chanted aisle to aisle, bed to bed. The dog barked. Uneasiness and distress filled the room. Jay lifted Paul's cat into his arms to keep the cat safe. Miss Thing stopped when she reached the hospital bed where Jay was standing with the cat. "Angry now?" she yelled at him. Cha Cha growled.

"Angry?" Jay answered. "Of course, I'm angry. And I'm also tired and depressed and numb."

"This could have been stopped. Prevented. The government ignored us."

"The government ignores a lot of things, which is why some of us are here to help."

"And the profits! I can't afford the medicine. And I can't afford the insurance that would get me the medicine."

"I don't think anyone affords this kind of treatment. Or can *afford* it."

"I've already lost Manny Q and Jada. I need someone to hear me."

"And I've lost buddies and clients and friends and lovers."

"Things need to change."

"I'm not the enemy."

"We must fight. Our voices need to be heard!"

"But this is not the place," Jay said. "This is not the time. This is not the moment for that."

Miss Thing stood silent, but refused to feel ashamed. She started chanting, "Where is your Rage? Where is your Rage?" And the group began to join her.

The chanting became louder. Several logs began to smoke out of despair. One of the chanters burst into flames and the smoke began to surround the crowd.

The smoke became thicker. Jay coughed. He knew evacuation was next. Cha Cha trembled and struggled to get away from Miss Thing.

"Cha Cha hates hospitals," Miss Thing whispered, trying to calm the dog. Paul's cat leapt out of Jay's arms. Jay flinched, uncertain where to go next. He tried to push the hospital bed but it was bolted to the floor. He tried to lift the body in the bed, but the log was too heavy and already smoking. He tried not to panic, calling into the smoke, "Hello! Hello! We need to find the exit! Now!"

Paul's cat darted to a doorway that led to a flight of stairs. The dog wiggled out from Miss Thing's arms and pursued the cat. Miss Thing chased the dog. Jay followed but kept looking back and calling out, "This way! This way out!"

Up to the Roof

The stairs were steep, the stairwell airless, a landing spot changing into an illogical direction or sometimes into a spiral. Jay tried to keep his neck up, his eyes looking ahead. Through another doorway, he reached the roof of the building. Ahead he saw Paul's cat, prancing along the black tar pavement as if it were hot, rubbing its side against a wall, then jumping up onto a ledge.

It was a dark evening. The air was warm and still. Lights surrounded the rooftop. Building windows lit. Reflections from street lights and traffic. The glimmer of neon signs. The cat sat contently on the ledge as if this was where he was headed all along.

"I'm sorry," he heard someone whisper. Jay turned, looked around, "Paul?"

"I'm sorry," he heard again.

Jay listened, waiting to hear it again, then said, "No. I'm sorry."

"Sorry," he heard again. This time he wasn't sure if it was Paul or someone else. There was no sign of Miss Thing and Cha Cha. Then he heard another "sorry." He said it again. "I'm sorry." Jay wasn't sure what he was sorry for. For living? For loving? For trying to be himself?

He felt unsteady, as if the roof was spinning. When he placed his hand against the ledge of the roof to balance himself, he saw tiny lights ascending the sky. Each seemed to twinkle and whisper "sorry."

It was beautiful. Magical. Enchanting. He watched the lights and whispers ascend into the dark blue evening sky. It was all the things being an adult in a big city should be. Beautiful and painful. Jay could only stand and watch and wish he was not alone. "Sorry," he said, and a tiny light left his lips and floated upward.

Jay watched. The cat sat atop the ledge respectfully. Then, it stretched and walked along the ledge. It stopped and looked at Jay.

Jay felt the stare of the cat. It was hard to look away from the lights and whispers. He noticed Miss Thing walk onto the roof. She carried Cha Cha in her shoulder bag. The cat scampered along the ledge and jumped onto Miss Thing's shoulder. Miss Thing did not react but Cha Cha growled from below.

"Kitty!" Jay said. He approached Miss Thing, his arms reaching out to take the cat. "Thank you! Thank you! I can take the cat back to the apartment."

"Not so fast," Miss Thing said. "You can't just take the cat. How do I know you're qualified?"

"Qualified? I need a license to save a cat?"

"The cat doesn't need saving. A cat chooses its friends. Why don't you know that?"

"I've never had a cat before."

"See? And you think you can just waltz in and everything will be okay."

"Everything is not okay," Jay said. "That's why I'm here. I know I am not the one the cat wants. I know I'm not Paul. I'm just doing what I think I should do. I'm just trying to help."

Miss Thing gave Jay a hard, fierce stare, but Jay could tell from her posture, the messy make up, that she was exhausted. "You got a name?" Jay asked.

"You know who I am."

"I mean your name. Your name name."

"Ernie," she answered. "Ernesto, really."

"It suits you."

"You remind me of my ex-boyfriend," she said.

"I hope that is a compliment," Jay replied.

"Yes and no."

"Why do you say that?"

"He didn't want to fight."

"We're not all fighters," Jay said. "Some of us are helpers. It helps me when I help someone."

"I get it," she said. "I get it now. We're alike. We just fight different."

Jay nodded. "I get it. I get it now." He looked at the cat. "Do I pass?"

"There was never any failure," Miss Thing said.

The dog sneezed and the cat jumped off of Miss Thing's shoulder to the ledge of the roof and sat. The cat stared at Jay to make sure that Jay was staring back. Then, the cat leapt down to the roof and headed to the doorway. It stopped and looked back at Jay to make sure he was following.

Jay wanted to ask Miss Thing one more question before he followed the cat. As he began to say, "Are you ...?" Miss Thing pressed her finger against Jay's lips to quiet him.

"Yes ..." she whispered and Jay felt a jolt pass through his body. The rooftop suddenly became bright. As his eyes adjusted Jay saw that he was back in the hallway, standing in front of Paul's door. The jolt had been the sound of the door lock unbolting and the vibration passing through the cold metal frame of the door to his hand and body.

Jay slipped the key out of the lock and knelt down so that when he pushed the door open, he could welcome and catch Paul's cat. He pushed the door slowly open, his eyes meeting the cat's as their faces came into view of each other.

The cat looked at Jay and seemed to welcome the company. The cat leapt up to Jay's knee and then onto his chest. Jay stood up and holding the cat, entered the apartment, closing the door behind them.

Jameson Currier

Jameson Currier is the author of eight novels, five collections of short fiction, and a memoir. His most recent books are his illustrated tales, *Paul's Cat, The Candlelight Ghost, Mr. Darcy's Pride, Half of Hamlet, The Theater Bug, Mister Nightingale,* and *The Man That Got Away.* In 2010, he founded Chelsea Station Editions and in 2011, he launched *Chelsea Station* magazine. A self-taught artist, illustrator, and graphic designer, Mr. Currier's design work is tagged as "Peachboy" and his original art is signed "Jimmy." In 2020, he established Chatham Junction Studio, which serves as the curator for his expanding body of original art. He currently divides his time between a studio apartment in New York City and a farmless farmhouse in the Hudson Valley.